YOU CAN!

PEOPLE SKILLS FOR LIFE

Why not use Allan Pease as guest speaker for your next conference or seminar?

PEASE INTERNATIONAL PTY LTD

PO Box 1260, Buderim 4556, Queensland, AUSTRALIA
Tel: +61 7 5445 5600

Email: info@peaseinternational.com
Website: www.peaseinternational.com

Allan and Barbara Pease are the most successful relationship authors in the business. They have written a total of 15 bestsellers - Including 9 number ones- and give seminars in up to 30 countries each year. Their books are available in over 100 countries, are translated into 51 languages and have sold over 25 million copies. They appear regularly in the media worldwide and their work has been the subject of 9 television series, a stage play and a number one box office movie which attracted a combined audience of over 100 million.

Their company, Pease International Ltd, produces videos, training courses and seminars for business and governments worldwide. Their monthly relationship column was read by over 20 million people in 25 countries. They have 6 children and 5 grandkids and are based in Australia and the UK.

Also by Allan Pease:

DVD Programs
Body Language Series
Silent Signals Series
How To Be A People Magnet - It's Easy Peasey
The Best Of Body Language
How To Develop Powerful Communication Skills - Managing the Differences Between Men & Women

Audio Programs
The Definitive Book Of Body Language
Why Men Don't Listen & Women Can't Read Maps
Why Men Don't Have A Clue & Women Always Need More Shoes
How To Make Appointments By Telephone
Questions Are The Answers
It's Not What You Say

Books
The Answer
Body Language-How to Read others Thoughts by their Gestures
The Body Language of Love
Body Language in the Work Place
The Definitive Book Of Body Language
Why Men Don't Listen & Women Can't Read Maps
Why Men Lie & Women Cry
Why Men Want Sex & Women Need Love
You Can! People Skills For Life
Questions Are The Answers
Why He's So Last Minute & She's Got It All Wrapped Up
Why Men Can Only Do One Thing At A Time & Women Never Stop Talking
How Compatible Are You? Your Relationship Quiz Book
Talk Language
Get It Write

www.PeaseInternational.com

YOU CAN!

PEOPLE SKILLS FOR LIFE

Allan & Barbara
PEASE

Manjul Publishing House

First published in India by

Manjul Publishing House

• 7/32, Ansari Road, Daryaganj, New Delhi 110 002
Website: www.manjulindia.com

Registered Office:

10, Nishat Colony, Bhopal 462 003 - India

Distribution Centres

Ahmedabad, Bengaluru, Bhopal, Kolkata, Chennai,
Hyderabad, Mumbai, New Delhi, Pune

This edition first published in 2007
Fifth impression 2017

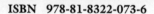

ISBN   978-81-8322-073-6

Printed and bound in India by Thomson Press (India) Ltd.

Acknowledgements

Here are some of the people who contributed directly or indirectly to this book, whether they knew it or not:

Ray & Ruth Pease, Dr Dennis Waitley, Trevor Dolby, Malcolm Edwards, Ron & Toby Hale, Deb Mehrtens, Jim Cathcart, Steve Wright, Trish Goddard, Kerri-Anne Kennerley, Bert Newton, Leon Byner, Ron Tacchi, Gerry & Kathy Bradbeer, Kathy Contoleon, Trevor Velt, Kevin Fraser, Alan Garner, Brian Tracy, Gerry Hatton, John Hepworth, Glen Fraser, David Smith, Sally & Geoff Burch, Dorie Simmonds, Decima McAuley, Ian & Jo Abbott, Norman & Glenda Leonard.

Contents

Introduction

We all admire those who seem to have the natural ability to enter an unfamiliar social situation and begin to engage others in conversation. These people have what is often called 'charisma'. While some people wonder how they do it, most assume that they must have a 'natural' talent. The reality is that 'charisma' is an acquired skill of influential people, and like any other acquired skill, it can be learned, enhanced and perfected when you have the right information and the determination to learn.

You Can! – People Skills for Life will provide you with the necessary skills you'll need to become influential with *everyone*. When you put these skills into action, don't be surprised if people begin asking, "Where did you get the ability to talk with people so successfully?" Even if they don't ask, they'll certainly be thinking about it, just as you once did.

This book is about the essential skills that achieve extraordinary success with everyone. We've designed it so that you can open it at any page and start learning a new skill instantly. You'll notice that we get straight to the point with each skill, give an example and then finish. Just like this introduction.

Allan & Barbara Pease

The Half Way House

A small Inn sat on the side of a picturesque Italian hill, half way between the cities of Venice and Verona. One night, a traveller checked in.

"Where are you travelling to?" asked the Innkeeper.

"I'm from Venice and am going to live in Verona" replied the traveller. "Tell me," he continued, "what are the people like who live in Verona?"

"Well – what were the people like in who live in Venice?" asked the Innkeeper.

"They're terrible people!" exclaimed the traveller, "they're uncaring, cold and distant. They'd never lift a finger to help anyone! That's why I left."

"Hmmmm . . ." muttered the Innkeeper, "then you won't like living in Verona . . . the people there are exactly the same!"

Disappointed at what the Innkeeper had said, the traveller retired to his room.

Later that night, another traveller checked in.

"Where are you travelling to?" asked the Innkeeper.

"I'm from Verona and am going to live in Venice" replied the second traveller. "Tell me," he continued, "the people who live in Venice - what are they like?"

"Well – what were the people like in Verona?" asked the Innkeeper.

"They're wonderful people!" exclaimed the traveller, "they are caring, warm, friendly and always helpful. I was sad to leave."

"Then you'll love living in Verona" said the Innkeeper, "The people there are exactly the same!"

THE MORAL
Others respond to you in the same way you treat them.

The Three Fundamentals of Human Nature

1. The Importance of Feeling Important

The greatest needs of human nature are to feel important, to be recognized and be appreciated

— Thomas Dewey

The human need to feel important has been found to be higher than physiological needs such as hunger because after a person has eaten, they are no longer hungry. The need for feeling important is even higher than the need for love because when love is attained, the need is satisfied. It's also higher than safety because when a person is secure, safety is not an issue.

The desire to feel important is the strongest constant human urge and is the one characteristic that separates us from the animals. It makes people want to wear brand label clothing, drive upmarket cars, have a title on their door or brag about their children. It's the main reason kids join street gangs. Some people will even become stalkers or murderers in their pursuit of notoriety.

Marriage studies have found that the prime reason women leave long term relationships is not because of abuse, cruelty or domination – it's because of lack of appreciation. The desire to be recognized, to feel important and appreciated is all-powerful. And the more important you make someone feel, the more positively they will respond to you.

2. People's Primary Interest is in Themselves

Others are far more interested in themselves than in you, so your main goal when talking with them is to talk about *them*.

You should talk about

their feelings
their family
their friends
their status
their needs
their opinions
their possessions

and never about *you* or *yours* – unless they ask.

In other words, on a basic level, people are only interested in themselves and 'what's in it for them'. To successfully relate to people, you must approach them with this rule being the basic foundation stone of human relations. And if someone doesn't ask about *you* and *yours*, they're simply not interested, so don't bring it up.

Some people are disappointed at this basic principle of human nature and see others as selfish and self-possessed because it's fashionable to believe that we should give of ourselves with no expectation of return. Most people who give completely selflessly understand the basic law that "what you give will be returned to you in some way, at some other time, plus interest." The reality is that every act we perform in life is motivated by self-interest. Even the donation you made to your local charity was motivated by self-interest and the feeling of generosity you felt when giving. The bottom line is that you received the ultimate payoff, even if you did it anonymously. Mother Teresa gave her entire life to others so that she could feel fulfilled in herself by making God happy. And all these actions are positive, not negative.

People who expect others to act in ways other than primarily for their own interests are continually disappointed and feel 'let down' by others.

There is no need to feel embarrassed about this or apologize for it – it's simply the way life is. Doing things for ourselves is a survival instinct that is hard-wired into our brains and has been a characteristic of humans since the beginning. It's the basis of self-preservation. Understanding that we all put our own interests first is one of the keys for any successful venture in dealing with others.

Practice making people feel important through recognition and appreciation every day for thirty days, and it will become a habit that will come naturally to you forever.

3. Nature's Law of Equal Returns

This is an irresistible subconscious urge to return to the giver, something of equal value to what was given. If a person likes what you give them, they will want to reciprocate by giving or doing something that you will like. For example, if a person receives a card from someone they haven't sent a card to, they feel an urge to quickly try to respond.

When you do someone a favor they will usually watch for the opportunity to reciprocate. If you pay someone a compliment, they will not only like you, they will try to return it. If you seem aloof or distant however, they will perceive you as unfriendly and they'll behave in an unfriendly way. If you are dismissive, you may be considered rude or glib and they'll respond to you in a similar way. If you insult them, they feel the urge to return the insult. But when you put out something positive, you will, at some point, receive a positive in return. When you put out a negative however, you will receive in return a much *greater* negative than you gave. This is a Law of Nature, and it rarely fails.

To be popular, always make people feel more important than you in some way. If you act as though you are better, they will feel inferior or jealous. This is counter-productive to building positive relationships.

For example, any time you are served an excellent meal at a restaurant, or a shop attendant asks how you are, or the cleaner at the airport takes away your dirty dishes, smile and make a point of thanking them for their courtesy.

When you understand and accept these three fundamental aspects, you will be amazed at the power you will have in influencing others.

Summary

1. **The highest urge of human nature is to feel important and to be appreciated**
    *   The more important you make someone feel, the more positively they will respond to you.

2. **People's primary interest is in themselves**
    *   Approach others from a position of what *they* think and what *they* want.

3. **Nature's Law of Equal Returns**
    *   Whatever you give out, you will receive back in multiples sometime, somewhere.

SECTION A

Making People Feel Important

1

How to Give Sincere Compliments

Research shows that when you compliment others, you are likely to be seen as sympathetic, understanding and attractive. So, compliment your partner, your colleagues, your employees, your boss, the person you just met, your customer or client, the postman, the gardener, your children. Everyone! There is something about *every* person that you can notice and compliment, however small or insignificant it may seem to you. We guarantee that if you regularly try to make everyone feel special, a new and different world will open up to you.

The most common way to express admiration is to deliver a Direct Positive compliment. This type of compliment tells someone, in a straightforward manner, what you appreciate about their *behaviour, appearance* or *possessions*.

For example:

Behaviour: You're a good trainer.
Appearance: You have a nice hairstyle.
Possessions: I like your garden.

Of these three compliments, a compliment about a person's behaviour has been shown to have the most persuasive effect. Compliments like these become powerful with two techniques:

1. Using the person's name

Using a person's name creates a greater level of interest in the conversation and causes them to listen intently to any statement that follows. Any time you make an important point, preface it with the listener's name and the attention given to that point and how much they remember are significantly increased.

2. The *What/Why* technique

Most compliments fail because they state *what* they like but don't explain *why* they like it. The power of the compliment depends on its sincerity; only telling the person *what* you like often sounds like flattery and doesn't work. Always say *why* you like it. For example:

> Behaviour: '_Alan_, you are a good trainer _because_ you give each of us your personal attention.'
>
> Appearance: '_Sue_, you have a nice hairstyle _because_ it highlights your eyes.'
>
> Possessions: '_John_, your garden is beautiful _because_ it blends perfectly with the environment.'

Become a name user, tell others *what* you like and *why* you like it and they will remember you and what you say for a longer period of time. Never pay a compliment if you really don't mean it. That's flattery and is easy to spot. Flattery is telling another person exactly what he thinks of himself.

Third-person Compliments

These are compliments intended to ultimately reach someone other than the person you are addressing. You can deliver a third-person compliment by making it within earshot of the person for whom it is intended. You can make the compliment to someone else such as a best friend or the local blabbermouth. In other words, to a person who is likely to pass it on. Praise delivered publicly this way is far more believable and more valuable than praise delivered privately.

Relayed Compliments

This compliment involves someone else mentioning that he likes the behaviour, appearance or possessions of another person, and you passing on that message.

For example:

"Hey _Bob_ – John tells me you're the best player in the club _because_ you're unbeatable. What's your secret?"

A business person calling a prospect on the telephone for an interview could say:

"_Mr. Johnson_, I hear you're the best accountant in town _because_ you get results. Is that true?"

This relieves tension and usually gets a laugh.

How to Receive a Compliment

When someone pays you a compliment:

1. Accept it
2. Thank them for it
3. Prove your sincerity

For example:

Kylie: "Your car looks nice, Anne."
Anne: "Thanks Kylie. I washed and waxed it this morning and your noticing makes me feel good! I appreciate it."

Accepting compliments shows others that you have a good self-image. Rejecting a compliment is usually interpreted as a personal rejection of the person giving it.

Make it a habit right now to compliment three people every day on their behaviour, appearance or possessions and watch how they react to you. You'll quickly discover that it's more rewarding to give compliments than it is to receive them.

2

How to Listen Effectively

We all know people who are good talkers, but we'd rather spend time with good listeners. A fascinating conversationalist is a person who listens intently whilst the other person is speaking.

Good listeners make better first impressions than good talkers. Forty percent of people who see a doctor do so because they want someone to listen to them, not because they're ill.

For the most part, angry customers, dissatisfied employees and upset friends simply want someone to listen to their problems.

To be a great conversationalist, be a great listener.

We can think three times faster than we can listen and that's why most people find it difficult to listen effectively. In business, the first step is to sell yourself and then to sell your idea, product, service or proposition. This stage is known as the 'listening stage'. You sell yourself first and then ask relevant questions about your prospects and their needs to uncover their dominant desires or 'Hot Buttons'.

The 5 Golden Rules for Listening

1. Use 'active listening'

'Active listening' is a remarkable way of encouraging others to keep talking and to be sure you understand what they are saying to you.

To use 'active listening' you simply paraphrase what a person says and feed it back to them, starting with the word 'you'.

Here's an example:

Mark: "My company has 1200 staff, so it's really tough to get ahead."

Melissa: "You're feeling really frustrated." (active listening)

Mark: "That's for sure. I go to the job promotion interviews but I don't seem to land the positions."

Melissa: "You think you're getting the run-around." (active listening)

Mark: "Exactly. If they don't think I'm up to it, I'd like to be told straight!"

Melissa: "You want others to be honest with you."

Mark: "That's right! And not only that...(etc.)"

If you're not sure that you've heard someone accurately, add the words, 'Am I right?' to the end.

For example:

Melissa: "You want others to be honest with you. Am I right?"

Active listening allows others to talk openly because you are not giving opinions or being critical. It also means that you are never wondering what to say next.

2. Use Minimal Encouragers

When the other person is speaking, encourage them to keep talking by using these Minimal Encouragers:

I see...
Uh, huh...
Really?
Tell me more...

Minimal Encouragers can triple the length of the other person's statements and the amount of information they give.

3. Keep eye contact with the person

Meet their gaze for the same length of time that they meet yours. Mirroring a person's gaze creates rapport.

4. Lean towards the person as you listen

We lean away from people we don't like or who bore us. Lean forward – show you're interested.

5. Don't interrupt the speaker; stick to the point

Avoid the urgency to change subjects. Let them finish what they're saying.

How to say 'Thank You'

To some people, learning how to say 'thank you' may seem trivial but it is one of the most powerful skills in the art of building relationships. Look for opportunities for thanking people wherever possible.

The Four keys for an effective 'Thank you'

1. Say your thanks clearly and distinctly

By speaking plainly you leave no doubt in the person's mind that you mean your thanks. Be glad you're saying it. When others overhear you giving thanks, it amplifies its effectiveness.

2. Look at the person and touch them

Making eye contact with the person reinforces your sincerity and a light brush on the point of their elbow with your hand will reinforce your thanks and make it more memorable.

3. Use the person's name

Personalize your thanks. "Thank you, Susan" is far more powerful than "Thank you".

4. Send a written 'thank you' note

This is the best 'thank you' when the situation allows for it. A face to face "thank you" comes next in impact, followed by a telephone 'thank you'. And a text message is better than saying nothing.

Be sincere when you thank a person. Let them know your thanks is genuine. If you're not honest about it, your body language will give you away. Become a 'Thank You' carrier. Look for opportunities to thank others about things that are not obvious.

4

How to Remember People's Names

To every person, their name is the sweetest sound in the world. To them it encompasses everything they are and studies show that people listen intently to any sentence following the use of their name.

Most of us don't remember people's names when we first meet them. This is because we are so preoccupied with the impression *we* are making that we don't even hear the person's name. It's not that we forget their names – we actually *don't hear* them.

Here are the 3 steps to developing powerful memory recall:

Step 1. Repeat their name

When you are introduced to someone new, say their name out loud twice to make sure you heard it correctly and this gives you the opportunity to memorize it. If you were introduced to Susan, say "Susan... nice to meet you, Susan." If it's an unusual name, ask them to spell it and this gives you even more time to memorize it.

Step 2. Turn their name into an object

The reason names are hard to remember is that they aren't solid objects that the mind can picture. To recall a person's name, make a picture in your mind of what their name sounds like. For example, 'Barbara' sounds like barbed wire, 'Jack' sounds like a car jack, for 'John' picture a toilet bowl and for 'Kathy' imagine a cat.

Step 3. Create a ridiculous scene

Next, imagine the object interacting in a ridiculous way with a prominent feature that the person has. For example, if Barbara has a larger than average nose, picture her with barbed wire through it and that you are leading her around with it. If Jack has a prominent chin, imagine a car jack under it jacking it up. If John (as in toilet) has a receding hairline, imagine he's wearing a toilet bowl on his head like a cowboy riding the range. If Kathy has three holes in her earlobes from wearing earrings, imagine a cat hanging from her ears by its claws. The secret is – the more ridiculous the scene, the easier it will be to recall.

Pages 20–22 give you a list of the 50 most common men's and women's names and the solid images to use for instant recall. Practice using these images and suddenly everyone will start to think you're a genius. Never tell anyone how you've become so great at recalling names, as you will quickly lose friends – especially when you meet Bruce (a goose) and Jennifer (chin of fur).

Memory keys for men's names

ADAM	A dam, Adam's Apple	JAMES	Jams
ADRIAN	A dream, A drain	JEFF	Deaf, chef
ALAN	Ale, a lens	JIM	Gym
ALBERT	A belt	JOE	Joke, joey
ALEX	Axe, legs	JOHN	Toilet
ANDRÉ	Entree	KEITH	Teeth, keys
ANDREW	Ant drew	KEN	Ken doll, can
ANTHONY	Ant eating honey, anthem	KEVIN	Heaven, cave in
ARNOLD	Arm hold	LARRY	Lairy, lariat
ARTHUR	Author	LOUIS	Louvres, lures
BARRY	Berry, bury	LUCAS	Low kiss
BEN	Bench, bend	LUKE	Luke warm
BERT	Bird	MALCOLM	Welcome, milk
BILL	$20 bill, duck bill	MARK	Marker, marking pen
BOB	Blob, English bobby	MATTHEW	Mat threw
BRIAN	Brain, iron	MIKE	Microphone
BRUCE	Bruise, goose	NEIL	Kneel, nail
CAMERON	Camera	NEVILLE	Never, Devil
CARL	Car, curl	NICK	A nick (cut), neck
CHARLES	Prince Charles, charred	PATRICK, PAT	Hat trick, pat
CHRIS	Xmas, Christ, cross	PAUL	Pole, pail
CLIFF	A cliff, cuff	PETER	Egg beater, heater, peat
COLIN	Collar, cold	PHILLIP	Phillips screwdriver, flip
DAMIAN	Dalmatian	RALPH	A barking dog, raf
DAN	Dance, den	REG	Red, reach
DARRYL	Drill	RICHARD	Rich Heart
DAVID	Davit, Star of David	RICK	Rickshaw
DENNIS	the Menace, dentist	ROBERT	Robber
DICK	Deck	ROBIN	Robin Hood
DON	Donald Duck, donkey	ROD	Rod, fishing rod
DOUG	Dig, dog	ROGER	Rager
DUNCAN	Dunk, dunnycan, dungeon	RONALD, RON	Ronald MacDonald, run
EDWARD	Head of wood	ROY	Royal, toy
EVAN	A van	SAM	Sandwich
FRANK	Frankenstein, frankfurter	SIDNEY	Opera House, sit knee
FRED	Fred Flintstone, frayed	SIMON	Sigh, Simple Simon
GARY	Carry, glory	STAN	Stand
GEORGE	Gorge	STEVE	Sleeve, steep
GERRY	Geriatric, jerry	TED	Dead, bed, Teddy bear
GRAHAM	Grey, grey ham	TIM	Dim (stupid), tin
GRANT	Granite	TOM	Tom cat, tom-tom drum
GREG	Keg, egg, grog	TONY	Toe knee
HARRY	Hairy	WARREN	Rabbit warren, warn
HENRY	Henry the 8th, hen	WAYNE	Whine, weighing
JACK	Car jack	ZACK	Sack

Memory keys for women's names

ABIGAIL	A big ale	JUDY	Judo
ADRIENNE	A drain	KAREN	Carrot
ALICE	Lice, Alice in Wonderland	KATE	Cake
AMANDA	Almond, A man	KATHY	Catty, cat
ANGELA	Angel	KAY	Key
ANITA	Ant eater	KIM	Kimono, Hymn
ANN	Ant, add	LAURA	Lord, lawn
ANNABEL	A new bell	LAVERNE	Love urn
ANNETTE	A net	LINDA	link, lint, lend
AUDREY	A tree	LISA	Leash, lizard
BARBARA	Barbed wire, barber	LOU	A loo, loop
BEATRICE	Beat rice	LOUISE	Leaves
BELINDA	Blind	LUCILLE	Loose ear
BEVERLEY	Beverage	LUCY	Loose
BRENDA	Blender	LYNDEL	Lentil
CARMEL	Caramel	MARJORIE	Margarine
CAROL	Carol, Xmas carol	MARTINA	Martini
CHARLOTTE	The harlot	MARY	Merry, marry
CHERYL	Cherry, chair	MAUREEN	Moron
CHRISTINE	Christen, Xmas	MAXINE	Maximum, Mad Max
CLAIRE	Eclair	MELISSA	Blister, miss her
CLAUDIA	Clawed, claws	MONICA	Harmonica
COLLEEN	Collar, clean	NICOLE	Nick, nickel
CRYSTAL	Crystal	OLIVIA	A lover
DAPHNE	Deaf knee	PAM	Pan
DAWN	Dawn	PAT/RICIA	Pat, pat of butter
DEBBIE	Debutante, deputy	PENNY	Pen, penny
DEBRA	The Bra	RACHEL	Rachet, rake
DENISE	Dentist, the knees	REBECCA	Beckon
DIANE	Dye, Lady Diane	ROBYN	Robin Hood
ELIZABETH	Queen Elizabeth, lizard	ROSEMARY	Rose, a merry rose
EMMA	Armour, hammer	ROXANNE	Rocks
EVELYN	A violin	SALLY	Salad
FIONA	Phoner, foamer	SANDRA	Sand
FLORENCE	Floor	SARAH	Sara Lee
GAIL	Gale	SERENA	Serene, screamer
HEATHER	Heaven, feather	SHIRLEY	Shirley Temple
HELEN	Hell, helmet	SONJA	Song, sonar
JACKY	Car jack, jockey	SOPHIE	Soapy, sofa
JAN	Jam	SUSAN	Soup, lazy susan
JANE	Chain	THERESA	Trees, Mother Theresa
JEAN	Jeans	VERONICA	Fur on her
JENNIFER	Chin of fur	VIRGINIA	Virgin
JESSICA	Chase a car	WENDY	Windy
JOAN	Joan Collins, joke	YVETTE	A vet

Memory keys for common last names

ADAMS	A dam	LAWSON	Law, lawman
ALLEN	Allen key, a lens	LEE	Lei, lay
ARMSTRONG	Strong arm	LEWIS	Louvres
BAKER	Baker, bakery	LIM	Limp, limb
BARNES	Barn	LYNCH	Lynching
BARRETT	Barrow, barrel	McDONALD	Ronald McDonald
BENNETT	Bonnett, bent it	MARSHALL	Marshall, sheriff
BLACK	Plaque	MARTIN	Martini
BRADY	Brandy, Brady bunch	MILLER	Miller, mill
BREWSTER	Rooster, brewery	MOORE	Mower
BROWN	Brown, brownie	MURPHY	Mercy, murky
BURKE	Burp	MURRAY	Marry, merry
BURNS	Burns, burner, sideburns	NEWMAN	New man (price a head)
CAMPBELL	Camp bell, camp	NORRIS	Nurse
CHANG	Chain, hang, shank	O'BRIEN	A brain
CLARK	Clerk, cloak, cluck	PAGE	Bool or magazine page
COLLINS	Joan Collins, collar	PARKER	Parking meter
COOK	Cook, Captain Cook	PEARCE	Pierce
COOPER	Copper, chicken coop	POWERS	Power fist, power tool
DAVIS	Davis cup, davits	PRESTON	Press, a ton-pressing
DICKSON	Duck's son, son of dick	RICHARDS	Rich heart
DOUGLAS	Dug, dog with glasses	ROBERTS	Robber, Robin Hood
EDWARDS	Head wood, head warts	ROGERS	Rods, Roy Rogers
EGAN	Eagle	RUSSELL	Wrestle
EVANS	Heavens	SCOTT	Scotsman
FOSTER	Frosty, Fosters Beer	SIMPSON	Shrimp, Samson
GALLAGAH	Galloper, galah	SINGH	Sing, sink
GRANT	Granite	SMITH	Blacksmith
GREEN	Golf green, greenhouse	STEELE	Steel bar, thief
GRIFFITHS	Grippers	STEWART	Stew, Steward
HAMILTON	Ton of ham	TAN	Suntan, tin
HARRIS	Hairless	TAYLOR	Tailor, tail
HENDERSON	Hen doors	THOMAS	Tom cat, Thomas train
HILL	Hill	TURNER	Tina, fitter and turner
HUGHES	Huge, hues	WAGNER	Wagon, wagging tail
HUNT	Hunk, hump	WALKER	A walker, the Phantom
JACKSON	Michael, car jack	WANG	Wham
JAMES	Jams	WASHINGTON	Washing machine
JOHNSON	Toilet (the John)	WATSON	Wet suit
JONES	Jokes, cones	WEST	Wild west, vest
KELLY	Gallery, Ned Kelly	WHITE	Wide
KENNEDY	Can of Tea	WILLIAMS	A will with arms
KING	King	WILSON	Whistle
KRAMER	Creamer	WOODS	Woods, warts
LAU	Loud	ZAMMIT	Summit

Summary

Technique 1. How to Give Sincere Compliments
- Compliment a person's behaviour, appearance or possessions.
- Say *what* you like and tell them *why* you like it.
- Begin with the person's name
- If someone compliments you, accept it, thank them and explain why you're grateful for the compliment.

Technique 2. How to Listen Effectively
- Use 'active listening'. Paraphrase what the person said and feed it back to them, starting with the word 'you'.
- Don't interrupt the speaker.
- Stick to the subject.
- Let them finish what they're saying.
- Use Minimal Encouragers.

Technique 3. How to say 'Thank You'
- Say your thanks clearly and distinctly.
- Look at and touch the person you're thanking.
- Use the person's name.
- Send a written thank you note

Technique 4. How to Remember Peoples' Names
- Repeat the name
- Turn their name into an object
- Imagine the object interacting in a ridiculous situation with their most prominent feature

SECTION B

How to Be a Great Conversationalist

5

How to Talk with People (and be extremely interesting)

People who are perceived as interesting talk about the other person's favourite subject – themselves. There are three ways to do this:

1. Be interested in others and encourage them to talk about themselves and their interests.

A person is more sincerely interested in the pimple on their nose than how many AIDS sufferers there are in Africa. You'll make more friends in 4 weeks being interested in others than you will in ten years of trying to get others to be interested in you.

2. Remove the words 'I, Me and Mine' from your vocabulary and replace them with 'You' and 'Yours'.

Instead of saying:

> 'I know how successful this plan is because **my** other clients tell **me** how **my** advice has helped achieve what they told **me** they wanted.'

Say:

> 'When **you** take this action **you'll** be excited about the results **you'll** achieve because it will benefit **you** and **your** family in ways **you** couldn't have imagined.'

3. Ask only questions that get them to talk about themselves

"How was **your** holiday?"

"How did **you** get started in **your** line of work?"

"How's **your** son going at his new school?"

"Who do **you** believe will win the next election?"

"What do **you** think about (whatever)?"

The Bottom Line – people are not interested in you or me – they are only interested in *themselves*. If you feel upset about this – get over it. Accept it as a fact of life.

6

How to Ask Great Questions

Most conversations have difficulty starting or continuing, not because of the things being discussed, but because the wrong type of questions are being used.

There are two types of questions you can ask:

1. Closed-Ended Questions

Closed-Ended questions ask for only a one or two word answer and make the conversation stop. For example,

Q: "When did you start work as an accountant?"
A: "8 years ago."
Q: "Did you like the movie?"
A: "Yes."
Q: "Who do you think will win the election?"
A: "The Liberals."

Closed questions make the conversation sound like an interrogation.

2. Open-Ended Questions

Open-Ended questions ask for explanations, opinions and elaborations and quickly build rapport with people because they show others that you're interested in them and what they have to say. People who ask Open-Ended questions are perceived as being interesting, sincere, dynamic and caring.

The four most powerful Open-Ended questions you can ask begin with:

How...?
Tell me about...
In what way...?
Why...?

Here are the same questions asked in an Open-Ended form:

Q: "**How** did you get started as an accountant?"
A: "When I was in school I was always interested in how numbers could influence outcomes... etc, etc."
Q: "**Tell me about** the part of the movie you enjoyed most?"
A: "I loved the scene where Dracula came through the door and said... etc, etc."
Q: "**In what way** do you feel the Labor candidate has influenced this election?"
A: "I've never voted for the Conservatives but I think that last night's debate could be the deciding factor because...etc, etc."

Practice asking only Open-Ended questions. If you ask a Closed-Ended question, immediately follow through with an Open-Ended one.

For example:

Q: "When did you move to Chesterville?" (Closed)
A: "About 10 years ago."
Q: "**Why** do you think Chesterville has changed so much in that time?" (Open)
A: "Well, when we first moved here there was not much development happening but five years ago the developers moved in and... etc."

7

How to Start a Conversation

People form up to 90% of their opinion about you in the first four minutes of meeting you so it's critical to have effective ways to start conversations in any situation. You have only three opening topics to choose from to start the conversation:

- the situation
- the other person
- yourself

and only three ways to begin:

- asking a question
- giving an opinion
- stating a fact

1. Talking about the Situation

Talking about the situation you are both in is usually the simplest and easiest way to start. Simply look around and ask an Open-Ended question about what you notice. This can be done anywhere, for example -

At a market: "I notice you're buying zucchinis. I've never known how to cook them. How do you prepare them?"

At an art gallery: "What do you think the artist was trying to say?"

At a meeting: "How did you happen to be at this meeting?"

In a line at a restaurant: "Why do you think this place is so popular?"

In a supermarket: "What do you think is the best way to use this detergent?"

Opening a business presentation: "How did you get started in this line of business?"

2. Talking about the Other Person

People love to talk about themselves and are happy to respond to any questions you ask about them.

At a party: "That's an interesting emblem on your jacket. What does it stand for?"

At a golf course: "You've got a great swing. How did you perfect it?"

At a meeting: "I notice you voted for redevelopment of the park. In what way do you think the park could be improved?"

At the beach: "I see you belong to the Lifesaving club. How does someone get started in that?"

3. Talking About Yourself

The rule here is simple – unless someone asks you a question about yourself, your family, your possessions or your occupation, they're simply *not* interested. When starting a conversation, never volunteer information about yourself unless someone asks.

8

How to Keep a Conversation Going

Use Bridges

People who give short answers to Open-Ended questions are best handled with a 'bridge' to keep them talking. Bridges in effect, are shortened versions of Open-Ended questions. They are best used with people who give brief answers to Open-Ended questions.

Bridges include:

Meaning..?
For example..?
So then..?
Therefore..?
Then you..?
Which means..?

The use of a bridge must be followed by silence on your part.

John: "How did you happen to move to this area?"
Martin: "I like the climate better."
John: *"Better than...?"*
Martin: "...better than the polluted air in the city."

John: *"Which means...?"*

Martin: *"...which means improved health for me and my family. In fact, I read a report the other day that said people's overall health was deteriorating and ... etc."*

In this example, John used two bridges; he has the ball rolling and doesn't sound like an interrogator. And he's not doing most of the talking.

You need to use two physical actions to use a bridge successfully:

1. Lean forward with your palm out when you say the bridge
2. Lean back and stop talking after using the bridge

Leaning forward with your palm out conveys that you are non-threatening and lets the listener know that it's his turn to talk by 'handing over' the control.

When you've used a bridge, *stop talking!* Resist the urge to add pearls of wisdom to the seemingly endless silence that can sometimes follow the use of a bridge. The outstretched palm gives the responsibility to speak next to the listener, so let him come up with the next statement. After you have given the control, lean back or sit back, put your hand on your chin and nod your head. This encourages the listener to keep talking.

Bridges are fun to use; they make conversations more productive and give you the power of silent control. When bridges are combined with Minimal Encouragers, they become some of the most dynamic tools you have in your bag to keep conversations going.

9

How to Keep Others Interested in your Conversations

Who makes more friends than anyone and is always accepted by every person he meets? The answer is – a dog. As soon as he sees you he wags his tail with excitement, thinks you're perfect in every way and is only interested in you and you alone. He never has a negative word to say about you, thinks you're a great singer and the later at night you come home, the more excited he is to see you.

He gives you unconditional love with no ulterior motives, no demands for compensation and doesn't want you to buy life insurance from him.

Only talk to people about the things that interest *them*, not the things that interest you. Most people only care about what *they* want and are interested in, and not in what you want.

You see, if you go fishing, there's no point in baiting your hook with something *you* like to eat like steak, hamburgers or chocolate ice-cream. Put something on the hook that the *fish* loves – a worm or a smelly prawn. This is the only way to influence others. Talk only in terms of what *they* want.

Most people are not effective or interesting when they talk with others because they only talk about *themselves* and their own needs.

You can only capture others' attention by discussing what *they* want and showing them *how* to get it.

10

How to Make People Feel Instantly Positive About You

Whatever facial expressions you send to others, they will send them straight back to you. Evidence shows that responding positively to a smiling face is hardwired into the brain. A smile communicates "I'm happy to see you and I accept you". This is why everyone loves constant smilers, like babies.

Professor Ruth Campbell, from University College, London, discovered a 'mirror neuron' in the brain which triggers the part responsible for the recognition of faces and expressions and causes an instant mirroring reaction. In other words, whether we realize it or not, we automatically copy the expressions we see.

In humans, smiling serves much the same purpose as it does with other primates. It shows another person you are non-threatening and asks them to accept you on a personal level. This response is also hardwired into the brain.

This is why smiling regularly is such an important habit to develop as a part of your body language repertoire, even when you don't feel like smiling, because it directly influences other people's attitudes to you and how they respond to you.

Frowning is a negative facial expression to have when talking with others because they perceive that you either don't like them or are critical of them. If you are a frowner, try putting your hand on your forehead when you talk, to train yourself out of this destructive habit.

Summary

When you smile at another person they will almost always return your smile. This causes positive feelings in you both because of cause and effect. Studies show that most encounters will run smoother, last longer, have more positive outcomes and dramatically improve relationships when you make a point of regularly smiling and laughing often. Practice this to the point where smiling becomes a habit.

Evidence also shows that smiles and laughter build your immune system, defend against illness and disease, medicate the body, sell ideas, attract more friends and extend life.

Humor heals.

Smile!

11

How to Empathize with People

Most people want others to empathize with them or their cause, and to feel understood. The FEEL-FELT-FOUND technique achieves this goal and makes people feel positive toward you. Rather than disagreeing with a complaint or grievance, you say:

> "I understand how you FEEL. I know someone who was in a similar situation to you and they FELT the same way. They FOUND that by (give your solution) they were able to reach a positive outcome."

If someone said:

> 'I can't do business with your organization because I hear your service is lousy',

you'd respond:

> 'I understand exactly how you FEEL. One of our long-standing and valued customers FELT exactly the same way. But, they FOUND that simply by placing their order before noon they received same day delivery.'

If Sue said:

> 'I don't think I love you Justin'

He could say:

'I know how you **FEEL** Sue. Jessica once **FELT** the same way about Paul, but when they sat down and discussed their situation, she **FOUND** that, deep down, Paul was really a caring, sharing guy.'

In both of these cases, you have not disagreed with the other person or argued the point. In fact, you almost sound as if you've agreed with them. Don't defend an attack from someone; acknowledge their feelings.

12

How to be Agreeable with *Everyone* (even those who criticize you)

Having an agreeable manner is one of the most important habits you can cultivate. People love those who are agreeable and dislike those who disagree. To be agreeable with anyone who is critical of you, either agree if it's true or agree with the critic's right to their opinion.

1. How to agree with the Truth

The most powerful response you can give to your critic is to agree with the truth of what they say and then restate your position.
    For example:

Mother: If you go dancing tonight, you'll have trouble getting out of bed for work in the morning.
Daughter: You're probably right! But I love dancing and can't wait to go!

The daughter has *agreed with the truth* of her mother's criticism, while at the same time maintaining her own position.

Sue: I don't think you should quit your job, Adam. You're a key person in the company and if the economy goes bad you'll still have a job. Going into business alone has no guarantees!

Adam: You're absolutely right, Sue. There are no guarantees but I know I'll do well and I'm really looking forward to this opportunity!

Adam agreed with the truth of what Sue said. He didn't argue with her or put himself or her down and he still maintained his position without being aggressive.

2. How to agree with your critic's right to an opinion

Often, you will disagree with your critic's opinion, but you can still agree with their right to have an opinion, however silly you think their opinion is.

For example:

David: If you keep on spending all your money on clothes Monica, you'll end up broke!

Monica: I understand how you might feel that way Dave, but I just love the feeling of having a lot of different outfits.

Leanne: How could you buy a Mazda, Glen? You know Toyotas are much better cars!

Glen: Your opinion is understandable, Leanne and – you're right – Toyotas are great cars, but I just love the feel of the Mazda!

Glen and Monica both agreed with their critic's right to an opinion – Glen also agreed with the truth – but neither backed away from their position or made the other person feel wrong. Even when you <u>totally</u> disagree with their criticism, there is usually a way of being agreeable while affirming what you believe to be the truth. You're goal should be to always make others feel right, even when you don't agree with them.

Here are the five keys to becoming an agreeable person:

1. Decide to be agreeable with every person you meet.
    Develop an agreeable nature and make others feel right.

2. Agree with the Truth.
    Let others know that you agree with something they said. Nod your head and say, 'Yes, you're right' or 'I agree with you'.

3. Agree with your critic's right to an opinion.
    Even when you think they are talking complete nonsense, acknowledge that it's OK for them to think that way while, at the same time, you restate what you believe to be true.

4. Admit it when you are wrong.
    People who admit fault are admired by others but most people prefer to deny, lie or lay blame. If you're wrong say:

    'I certainly got that wrong ...'
    'I really blew it ...'
    'I was wrong ...'

5. Avoid arguing.
    You can rarely win an argument, even if you're right. Arguing loses friends and credibility and gives fighters what they want – a fight.

13

How to Create Positive 'Vibes' About Yourself

People form up to 90% of their first opinion about us in under four minutes and their initial evaluations of us are based primarily on our Body Language. Next, they listen to how we speak and what we say, then they determine their level of respect for us and their interest in us.

To command other's admiration and respect early in an initial meeting, do the following three things:

1. Be positive of who you are and what you do

Talk in glowing terms about your station in life and why you like it. Never put yourself down by saying things like, 'I'm just a clerk, only a housewife, etc.' Instead say, 'I work for the country's biggest bank helping people realise their investment goals' or, 'I'm the mother to two beautiful children and a life partner to John'.

If you can't be positive about who you are, neither can anyone else.

2. Be Enthusiastic

Talk about life with positive expectancy. Not only will this sell you to others, they'll also become enthusiastic about you and your conversations. Always smile – it makes people wonder what you've been up to.

3. Don't criticize anyone or anything

When you criticize, it is decoded by others as low self-esteem, lack of understanding or your lack of self-confidence. If someone mentions a competitor, praise the competitor's good points. If you can't say something positive, don't say anything. Don't try to build yourself up by knocking someone else down.

14

How to Make it Easy for People to say 'Yes'

Here are four ways to help a person say 'yes' to your proposal –

1. Find a reason for them to say 'yes'

Everything we do and any course of action we choose in life is motivated by a specific reason. Sometimes there are several reasons for doing something but there is always one dominant reason and this is what you need to uncover. By asking, 'What is your number one priority?' and listening to the answer without interruption, the other person will give you the reasons why they would be motivated to take action. Never assume you know a person's main reason for doing something, because you may be wrong and they won't feel motivated to take action. Never give a person *your* personal reasons for doing something unless your reasons are identical to theirs. When you uncover what *they* want, show them how they can get it using *your* solution. People are more persuaded toward the things they discover themselves rather than you telling them about it. Let them work out their problems themselves. All you need to do is ask the right questions that lead them to the right conclusion. As you explain your solution, replay the exact words *they* said about their number one priority.

2. Ask only 'yes' questions.

Open conversations by asking questions that can only be answered with a 'yes'. Avoid questions that will result in a 'no' answer.

Here are some examples of 'yes' questions:

> 'Are you interested in making money?'
> 'Would I be right in saying you want your family to be happy?'
> 'Would you like to spend more time with your children?'

Make their meeting with you a positive 'yes' experience and they will find it difficult to say 'no' to you later on. When influencing others, remember that your objective is to prove them right, not wrong – even if you don't agree with their point of view.

3. Nod your head

When we feel positive, we nod our heads. Research shows that if you *intentionally* nod your head, you'll experience positive feelings. Nod your head as you ask your 'yes' questions or as you listen to their responses, and watch how others *also* begin to nod their head and start to feel positive about your proposals.

4. Offer them a choice between two 'yeses'

When you offer only one option, the other person is forced to decide between 'yes' and 'no' – and 'no' is usually the option chosen by most people because it's safe. Offer a choice between two things you want them to do.

For example:

> 'Would it be better to meet you at 3pm or would 4pm be better?'
> 'Do you like the green – or is the blue better?'
> 'Will you use a credit card or would cash be more suitable?'
> 'When will you start – Wednesday or Thursday?'

15

How to Talk so Men will Listen

Research has shown that men use a specialized set of rules for communication with each other. If you are female, it's very important to understand these rules and abide by them when dealing with any male.

Here are the rules of 'Manspeak', formulated from the results of brain scans that track the blood flow and function of the male brain:

1. Give a man one thing at a time

Men's brains are compartmentalized. It's as if a man's brain is divided into little rooms with each room containing a function that works in isolation of all others. Do not multi-track with a man. Keep your ideas and thoughts separated. Deal with one thing at a time.

2. Let him have his turn to speak

Male brains are wired to either speak <u>or</u> listen. Most men can't do both simultaneously and this is why men take turns to talk. Let him have his turn and let him finish his sentence. Do not interrupt.

3. Use a poker face when listening

Men think that someone who uses many facial expressions when listening may have mental or emotional problems. Hold a serious expression when listening to a man and make listening sounds like, 'uh-huh…', 'I see…', 'hmmm…', 'Yeah, yeah…' to encourage him to continue.

4. Give him facts and information

Male brains are organized for spatial tasks and are interested in the relationship between things. Show solutions to problems, give facts and testimonials. Avoid emotional pleas. Instead, prove your point.

5. Use direct speech

Men's sentences are shorter than women's and contain more facts, data, information and solutions. Don't hint or infer things. Say what you mean and get to the point.

16

How to Talk so Women will Listen

Research has shown that women have a specialized set of rules for communication with each other. If you are male, it's vital that you understand these rules and comply with them when dealing with any female.

Here are the rules of 'Womanspeak', formulated from the results of brain scans that track the blood flow in the female brain:

1. Participate in the conversation

Don't wait for your turn to talk. Female brains are wired to both speak *and* listen simultaneously, which is why women often seem to all talk at the same time. This is because they <u>can</u>. If you wait for your turn you'll just get older. If you don't actively participate in a conversation with women, it is perceived as a lack of interest by you or that you hold a critical opinion.

2. Use facial expressions when listening

A woman's facial expressions reveal her emotions so, as she talks, mirror her expressions and gestures to create rapport. Never do this with a man.

3. Give her personal details and appeal to her emotions

Female brains are organized for reading the emotions of others and for evaluating relationships between people. Reveal to her, personal information about yourself and your family and volunteer your personal feelings about things.

4. Use indirect speech

Women's spoken sentences are longer than men's and may contain several subjects including her feelings and emotions about those subjects. Avoid getting to the point quickly, pushing for a fast solution to a problem, or 'closing the sale'. Be more friendly, relaxed and agreeable.

17

The 17 Powerless Phrases you Must Remove from Your Vocabulary

This is a list of some of the most damaging words and phrases you can speak. These phrases appear to say one thing while they in fact reveal the emotions, feeling and prejudices of the speaker. Eliminate them from your own vocabulary because they detract from your credibility.

What is said	What is heard
Kind of… Sort of thing…	You're not confident or don't know what you're talking about
You know what I mean…	You're unsure of what you're saying
The wife/husband/partner	Depersonalization of your partner
Truthfully Frankly Honestly Sincerely Believe me	People who are about to be dishonest, insincere, exaggerate or tell a lie often begin sentences with these words
Of course	You're trying to force agreement
Should/Ought	You're trying to force agreement through guilt or a sense of duty
Don't get me wrong	You're about to say something negative or critical

What is said	What is Heard
In my humble opinion…	You're about to make an egotistical statement
I don't want to be…	That's what you really want to be; e.g 'I don't want to be rude' is followed by a rude statement
I'll try	I don't expect to succeed
I'll do my best	My best isn't good enough
With respect	I have no respect for you

Be aware of these powerless words and phrases and make a point of eliminating them from your vocabulary.

18

The 12 Most Powerful Words You Can Use

A study at the University of California showed the most persuasive words in spoken language are:

discovery, guarantee, love, proven, results, save, easy, health, money, new, safety, you.

The new results you'll get from the discovery of these proven words will guarantee you more love, better health and will save you money. They're completely safe, and easy to use.

Practice these words and make them a normal part of your everyday conversations.

19

Turn Negative Statements into Positives

You can almost always find a way to turn destructive criticism into constructive praise. Instead of criticizing others for failing, you can compliment them for trying or for improving in some small way.

Consider these examples:

Instead of saying...	You could say...
Too bad you didn't get the pay rise	Barbara, I think it's great that you told your boss what you want, even if you didn't get it. What do you suppose you can do next to change his mind?
That story you wrote is ridiculous	Valerie, I like the paragraph where Burt is being forced to either marry or walk the plank because the words you used make it come alive for me. Where did you get the idea for that scene?
It took you five attempts to pass the test? What was the problem?	You stuck it out, Bill. Not everyone could have done that. What are you doing to celebrate?
You bombed out again! Guess you'll have to wait a few more months before you can start again.	Congratulations, Sue. You walked a step further than you did yesterday!

20

How to Deal with Fear and Worry

Studies have shown that of all the things we worry about in life:

87% never happen
7% actually occur
6% you will have some influence over the outcome

This means that most things in life that you worry about won't happen and that you have little to no control over the few things that do happen. So it doesn't pay to worry about the things you fear.

Approach fear for what it really is –

False
Evidence
Appearing
Real

Fear is nothing more than a physical reaction to thinking about the consequences you don't want. Most of your worries will never come to pass anyway, so they are nothing more than

False Evidence Appearing Real.

Never think about what you *don't* want to happen. Only think about what you *do* want, regardless of the outcome of a situation. What you think about is what you'll usually get.

Summary

Technique 5. How to Talk with People
- People are primarily interested in *themselves*.
- Remove the words 'I, Me and Mine' from your vocabulary and replace them with 'You' and 'Yours'.

Technique 6. How to Ask Great Questions
- Ask Open-Ended questions. Begin with: 'How?', 'Why?', 'In what way?', 'Tell me about…'

Technique 7. How to Start a Conversation
- Start the conversation by talking about either the situation or the other person
- Open with a question.

Technique 8. How to Keep a Conversation Going
- Use bridges such as: 'For example?', 'So then...?', 'Therefore?', 'Then you…?', 'Which means…?'

Technique 9. How to keep Others Interested in your Conversations
- Discuss only what *they* want and show them *how* to get it using your solutions.

Technique 10. How to Make People Feel Instantly Positive about You
- Smile at everyone. A smile communicates "I'm happy to see you and I accept you".

Technique 11. How to Empathize with People
- Tell others you know how they FEEL and that others have FELT the same way. Then explain the solutions they FOUND.

Technique 12. How to be Agreeable with *Everyone*
- Agree with the Truth of a criticism.
- Agree with the critic's right to an opinion.

Technique 13. How to Create Positive 'Vibes' about Yourself.
- Be positive of who you are and what you do.
- Be enthusiastic when you speak.
- Don't criticize anyone or anything.

Technique 14. How to Make it Easy for People to say 'Yes'
- Find a reason for them to say 'yes'.
- Ask only 'yes' questions.
- Nod your head when speaking and listening.
- Offer a choice between two 'yeses'

Technique 15. How to Talk so Men will Listen
- Give a man one thing at a time.
- Give facts and information.
- Let him have his turn to speak.
- Hold a poker face and use listening sounds when listening.
- Use direct speech.

Technique 16. How to Talk so Women will Listen
- Participate in the conversation. Don't wait for your turn.
- Use facial expressions while listening.
- Give personal details and appeal to her emotions.
- Don't push too early for solutions or conclusions.
- Use Indirect Talk. Don't be pushy.

Technique 17. The 17 Powerless Phrases to Remove
- Remove phrases and words that detract from your credibility, including – Kind of, Sort of thing, You know what I mean, The wife/husband/partner, Truthfully, Honestly, Frankly, Sincerely, Believe me, Of course, Should, Ought, Don't get me wrong, In my humble opinion, I don't want to be , I'll try, I'll do my best, With respect.

Technique 18. The 12 Most Powerful Words to Use
- The 12 most important words you can use are – discovery, guarantee, love, proven, results, save, easy, health, money, new, safety, you.

Technique 19. Turn Negative Statements into Positives
- Find a way to turn destructive criticisms into constructive praise.

Technique 20. How to Deal with Fear and Worry
- Almost everything you worry about won't happen and you have little control over the few things that will. So don't worry about everything.
- Approach fear for what it mostly is – **F**alse **E**vidence **A**ppearing **R**eal.

SECTION C

Giving Business Presentations

21

How to Make Lasting First Impressions

First impressions are the 'love-at-first-sight' of the business world. Here are the Nine Golden Opening Moves:

1. **Your Entry:** When you are invited to enter a room, walk in without hesitation. Do not stand in the doorway like a naughty schoolchild waiting to see the headmaster. People who lack confidence change gears and perform a small shuffle as they enter a room. Walk through the door with purpose and maintain the same speed.

2. **Your Approach:** Walk briskly. Influential people and those who command attention walk briskly at a medium pace with medium length strides. People who walk slowly or take long strides convey that they have plenty of time on their hands, are not interested in what they are doing or have nothing else to do.

3. **The Handshake:** Keep your palm straight (vertical) and return the grip pressure you receive. Let the other person decide when to end the handshake. Never shake hands directly across a desk as it can leave the other person having the 'Upper Hand' over you.

4. **Your Smile:** Make sure your teeth are visible when you smile, and smile with your whole face, not just your mouth.

5. **The Eyebrow Flash:** This is an ancient acknowledgement signal that is hardwired into the brain to be sent and received by others. Simply raise your eyebrows for a split second as you acknowledge the person.

6. **When you talk:** Use a person's name twice in the first 15 seconds and never talk for more than 30 seconds at a time. Speak at a slightly slower pace than they speak.

7. **When you sit:** If you are compelled to sit in a low chair directly facing the other person, turn away to an angle of 45 degrees to the person to avoid being caught in the 'reprimand' position. If you can't angle your chair, angle your body away.

8. **Your Gestures:** People who are cool, calm and in control of their emotions use clear, uncomplicated, deliberate movements. High status individuals use fewer gestures than low status individuals. Don't raise your hands higher than your chin. To create rapport, mirror the other person's gestures and expressions when appropriate.

9. **Your Exit:** When you're finished, pack your things calmly and deliberately – not in a frenzy – shake hands if possible, turn and walk out. If the door was closed when you entered, close it behind you as you leave. People watch you from behind as you leave so if you're a man, make sure the back of your shoes are shined. Hidden cameras show that, if you're a woman, others study your rear as you depart – whether you like it or not. When you get to the door, turn around slowly and smile. It's better that they recall your smiling face than your rear end.

22

How to Handle Criticism in Business

If a client or potential customer criticizes you or your organization, use the 'Put the Boot on His Foot' technique to diffuse the situation. Simply ask the person what *they* would do if they were in your situation and someone gave *them* the same criticism.

Whatever they say, you respond with:

"That's right! That's what we did!" or, "You're right! And that's what we're going to do!"

For example:

Prospect: "I've heard your delivery time is poor."

You: "Yes, it's true that we had some problems at our warehouse at one stage. Tell me, if you were the manager of a company that received that criticism, what would you do?"

Prospect: "I'd call a meeting of everyone concerned and work out a solid plan that would *guarantee* deliveries were made on time!"

You: You're absolutely right! And that's exactly what we did."

You have *agreed with the truth* and made your prospect feel right by stating that, not only is his opinion correct, your company has already taken it on board (or intends to take it). When you 'Put the Boot on His Foot', your prospect's objection becomes deflated and he won't feel the urge to raise it again.

If your company hasn't made the necessary changes to fix the problem then you don't deserve the prospect's business.

The Most Commanding Way to Answer the Telephone

Most people answer the telephone like this:

"XYZ Corporation... Allan speaking."

If you were walking toward someone, you wouldn't say "I'm Allan, walking.' On the phone it's obvious to the caller that you're speaking so don't say the word '*speaking*'.

Research shows that a person will recall the last word they hear when you answer the phone, so say your **name** last and use a Rising Terminal. A Rising Terminal is where you raise the volume and inflection of your voice. Studies show that when you do this, 86% of callers can recall your name versus 6% who can recall it when you answer with 'Allan *speaking...*'

From today, answer the telephone:

"XYZ Corporation... This is Allan."

and use a Rising Terminal on your name. This also prompts the caller to give you their name and a relationship can be immediately established. By the way, use *your* name, not Allan's.

How to Give a Reprimand or Critique

There are times when you, as a leader, will need to bring someone to account or point out behaviors that are unacceptable or non-productive. Most of us dread the thought of giving someone corrective action or discipline. The following 6-part technique can make it quick, powerful and painless for all concerned.

The 6 Golden Rules for a successful critique, reprimand or appraisal

1. Use the 'Sandwich Technique'

Onions taste bitter when eaten alone but can taste good when mixed with other salad items. To soften the blow, praise the person for something positive that he has done. Then deliver the criticism followed by another positive point about his performance.

2. Criticize the act, not the person

Explain that you are happy with him personally (assuming that's true!) but not with what he did.

3. Ask for their help

Never demand that a person 'does as they're told'. Say you need their co-operation and help to solve a problem.

4. Admit that you've made similar mistakes, and give the answer

Begin a criticism by talking about a similar mistake you've made in the past. This makes your criticism more digestible, just like a dentist giving anesthetic before drilling a person's teeth. Explain that you (and others) have had similar challenges to deal with in the past and show how you fixed the problem. When you admit that you are not perfect, others are influenced to follow your lead.

5. Make the criticism once, and do it in private

Never reprimand a person in front of others. Do it behind closed doors in a calm way and only mention the offence and its solution once. Do not keep hammering away about the person's poor performance.

6. End on a friendly note

Thank them for their co-operation in solving the problem and say that you look forward to seeing them deal with things in the new ways you have both discussed.

25

How to Give a Persuasive Speech

People who can stand and give a powerful, motivational talk are admired by everyone and are promoted into leadership positions both in business and socially.

Here is a four-step formula for giving a motivational speech 'off the top of your head' on any topic, whether it's for two minutes, twenty minutes or an hour. Memorize the following four points:

1. Ho-Hum
2. Why bring that up?
3. For example?
4. So what?

1. Ho-Hum

When you first stand to speak, the audience is silently thinking, 'Ho-hum… another dull speaker' so you must open with a dramatic, riveting or humorous story, statement or line that jolts the audience out of their complacency and grabs their attention.

2. Why bring that up?

Your next step is to tell them why you made the dramatic/humorous/riveting statement or story and why it is important to them.

3. For example?

This is where most of the body of your talk will be. Give three points or reasons about why what you're saying is true and important to them. When giving a longer talk, give three supporting points for each of your main three points.

4. So what?

At the end of your speech, your audience may be thinking, 'So, what do you want me to do about it?' and this is where you motivate them to embrace the ideas, thoughts or course of action you're suggesting.

Let's say, for example, you've been asked to talk to a group of parents about road safety and your objective is to convince them to use the pedestrian crossing and not walk randomly with their children across the busy road. Here's how you'd deliver it:

1. Ho-Hum

"Two thousand, three hundred and fifty-five children were needlessly crippled or had their lives cut short last year – and their parents are to blame. Statistically, two of you in this room will soon be looking into the eyes of a hospitalized child and praying that things will be alright. The question is – who of you will it be?"

2. Why bring that up?

"I bring up these statistics, ladies and gentlemen, because that's how many children were hit by cars in this country last year while crossing the road to meet their parents. And 96% of these children were not on a pedestrian crossing. What I am about to say is critical to each of you in this room. And that's because you love your children."

3. For Example?

(*Point 1*) "The National Safety Council conducted a study outside 46 schools recently and discovered ..." (back up your first point by quoting facts, statistics and other data).

(*Point 2*) "We conducted our own survey of parent's attitudes to road safety in our own neighborhood and found ..." (prove your second point).

(*Point 3*) "As a parent myself – and I know most of you have felt this same way – I have asked myself many times ..." (your third point, perhaps involving a personal, emotional opinion).

4. So what?

"So here's what I want you to do. From today, the next time you pick up your child from school, I want you to ..." (motivate your audience to do what you suggest).

When you've finished your talk, shut up and sit down.

Never thank the audience for listening to you – if you've done a good job, they should be thanking you.

26

How to Use a Visual Presentation

Research shows that when you are giving a visual presentation using books, charts, graphs or a laptop, 82% of the information is absorbed via the eyes, 11% via the ears, and 7% through the other senses.

Tell, show and involve

The Wharton study in the United States found that the retention of information from verbal presentations was only 10%. By comparison, the retention rate of a combined verbal and visual presentation is 51%. This means you can achieve a 400% increase in efficiency with the use of visual presentation aids.

The study also found using a visual aid can cut the average business meeting time from 25.7 minutes to 18.6 minutes – a 28% time saving.

But when however, we present our story using verbal, visual and emotional involvement, a person's retention rate rises to 92%.

We retain:

> 10% of what we hear
> 51% of what we see <u>and</u> hear
> 92% of what we see <u>and</u> hear <u>and</u> become involved in

So, when you only say it, it has the least effect. Telling *and* showing has a moderate effect. Telling, showing and getting others involved as you present gives the maximum retention.

Use the Power Lift

Use a pen to point to your presentation while at the same time, verbalise what the other person sees. Next, raise the pen from the presentation and hold it between his eyes and your eyes. This is called the *Power Lift* and has the magnetic effect of lifting his head so that he is looking directly at you and can *see* and *hear* what you are saying. This helps achieve a higher absorption of your message than from just talking. Keep the palm of your other hand visible when you are speaking.

Hold stronger eye contact with men when presenting your story but less frequently with women. If you're uncertain, mirror the amount of eye contact the other person gives you.

27

How to Decide Where to Sit in an Interview

Certain strategies using chairs and seating arrangements can create both persuasive or negative moods in an office or home.

There are five positions you can take at a rectangular table. Assume you are person B and the other person is A. You can choose any one of 5 positions to sit.

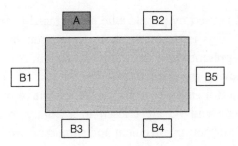

The Competitive/Defensive Position (B3)

The table becomes a solid barrier between both parties. Sitting across from a person can create a defensive, competitive environment and can lead to each party taking a firm stand on his own point of view.

Research into business encounters found that 56% of people perceive this position as competitive. In a business setting, this position is taken by people who are either competing with each other or if one is reprimanding the other. People who sit opposite speak less, are more negative, competitive or aggressive. If you are compelled to sit here, angle your chair to 45 degrees away from person A.

The Co-operative Position (B2)

When two people are thinking alike or both working on a task together, this position often occurs. The studies found that 55% of people chose this position as the most co-operative place to sit or intuitively sat there when asked to work jointly with another person. It is one of the best positions for presenting your story and having it accepted. It also allows for good eye contact and the opportunity for mirroring the other person's body language.

The Corner Position (B1)

This position is used by people who are engaged in friendly, casual conversation. This is the most strategic position from which you can deliver a presentation, assuming that person A is the audience. By simply moving the chair to position B1 you can relieve a tense atmosphere and increase the chances of a positive outcome.

Positions B4 and B5 are chosen in a library to communicate independence or non-involvement and should be avoided for giving presentations.

If you're invited to sit in an informal area of a person's office or home, such as at a round coffee table, it's a positive signal because 95% of business rejections are delivered from *behind* a desk. Never sit in a low sofa that sinks so low it makes you look like a giant pair of legs topped by a small head. If necessary, sit upright on the edge of the chair so you can control your body language, and angle your body to 45 degrees away from the person.

28

Ten Winning Body Language Strategies That Give You the Edge

As we've stated, people form up to 90% of their opinion about you in under 4 minutes and 60% – 80% of the impact you will make on them is non-verbal. The following ten strategies will give you the best opportunity to make a positive effect on others.

1. Keep Your Palms Up

Keep your palms visible when you talk. The response to this ancient signal is hard-wired into the brain. They will read you as non-threatening and will respond positively to you.

2. Keep Your Fingers Together

People who keep their fingers closed and their hands below their chin when they talk command the most attention. Using open fingers or having your hands held above the chin is perceived as less authoritative.

3. Keep Your Elbows Out

Sitting with your elbows on the armrest of a chair is perceived as a position of power and conveys a strong, upright image. Humble, defeated individuals let their arms drop inside the arms of the chair and they keep their elbows close to their bodies to protect themselves. They are perceived as fearful or negative, so avoid sitting like this.

4. Keep Your Distance

Respect the person's personal space, which will be greatest in the opening minutes of a new meeting. If you move in too close, the person may respond by sitting back, leaning away or using gestures that reveal their irritation, such as drumming their fingers or clicking a pen. Sit closer to familiar people but further back from new ones. Sit closer to those of similar age and further back from significantly older or younger ones.

5. Mirror Their Body Language

Mirroring the other person's body language and speech patterns builds rapport quickly. In a new meeting with someone, mirror his sitting position, posture, body angle, gestures, facial expressions and tone of voice. Before long, they'll start to feel that there's something about you they like – they'll describe you as easy to be with.

When presenting to couples, watch for who mirrors whom to uncover the decision-maker. If the woman makes the initial movements and the man copies, there is little point in asking him for a decision.

6. Match Their Speech Rate

A person's speed of speaking reveals the rate at which their brain can analyze information. Speak at the same rate or slightly slower than the other person and mirror their inflection and intonation. Studies show that others describe feeling 'pressured' when someone speaks faster than they do.

7. Uncross All Arms

Arms folded across the chest is an attempt to put a barrier between the person and something they don't like. A person's recall of what was said decreases by up to 40% when they fold their arms. Change someone's folded-arms position by handing them something to hold or giving them something to do. Give them a pen, book, brochure, sample or written test to encourage them to unfold their arms and lean forward. To be persuasive, *never* cross your own arms in any face to face meeting.

8. Touch Their Elbow

Mirror the touch you receive. If they don't touch you, leave them alone. Experiments however, have found that when a person is touched lightly on the elbow for not longer than three seconds, they are 68% more likely to be co-operative than if they weren't touched at all.

Studies show that female waitresses who were taught to touch the elbows and hands of their dining customers made 80% more tips from male diners than the non-touching waitresses, while male waiters increased their earnings by 32% regardless of which sex they touched. In other words, skilful elbow and hand touching can give you up to three times the chance of getting what you want.

9. Repeat Their Name

When you next meet someone new and you shake hands, extend your left arm, give a light touch on their elbow or hand as you shake and repeat their name to confirm you heard it correctly. Not only does this make the person feel important, it lets you remember their name through the repetition.

10. Avoid Touching Your Face

Studies show that when someone is concealing information or lying, their nose and face touching increases dramatically due to an increase in blood pressure when lying. Even if you have an itchy nose, people who don't know you may think you're lying. So keep your hands away from your face.

Practice It All

Before you go to an important interview or meeting, sit quietly for a few minutes and mentally rehearse the abovementioned things, seeing yourself doing them well. When your mind can see them clearly, your body will be able to carry them out. You need to cast yourself into a believable role in an interview, so practice mentally, in advance, how you will act, if you want others to take you seriously.

Evidence shows that, with practice, these skills will soon become second nature to you and serve you well for the rest of your life.

Summary

Technique 21. How to make Lasting First Impressions
- When you enter a room, walk in briskly, without hesitation.
- Keep your handshake vertical and return the grip you receive.
- Smile. Show your teeth and smile with your whole face.
- Raise your eyebrows for a split second.
- Use the person's name twice in the first 15 seconds.
- Angle your body to 45 degrees away from the other person.
- Use clear, uncomplicated, deliberate movements and gestures.
- Pack your things calmly and deliberately when you exit. If you're a woman, turn and smile as you leave.

Technique 22. How to Handle Criticism in Business
- 'Put the Boot on His Foot' and ask the person what he would do if he was in your situation and someone criticized his company.

Technique 23. The Most Commanding Way to Answer the Telephone
- Make your name the last word the caller hears and use a Rising Terminal.

Technique 24. How to Give a Reprimand or Critique
- Use the 'Sandwich Technique'
- Criticize the act, not the person
- Ask for their help
- Admit that you once made a similar mistake and give the solution
- Make the criticism once, and do it in private
- End on a friendly note

Technique 25. How to Give a Persuasive Speech

- Ho-Hum – open with a dramatic, riveting or humorous story, or statement.
- Why bring that up? – tell your audience why you made the statement and why it's important to them.
- For example? – give three powerful points and three supporting points for each main point.
- So what? – motivate your audience to take the action you're suggesting.

Technique 26. How to Use a Visual Presentation

- Showing people things and getting them involved as you present ensures the maximum retention of what is said
- Use the *Power Lift* to raise their eyes so they can *see* and *hear* what you're presenting

Technique 27. How to Decide Where to Sit in an Interview

- Avoid the Competitive/Defensive sitting position.
- Jockey for the Co-operative or Corner Positions

Technique 28. Body Language – Ten Strategies that Give You the Winning Edge

- Keep your palms visible
- Keep your fingers together
- Keep your elbows out
- Keep your distance
- Mirror their body language
- Match their speech rate
- Uncross all arms
- Touch their elbow
- Repeat their name
- Avoid face touching

Conclusion

How to Train an Elephant

Have you ever noticed how circus elephants are tethered by a light chain that is attached to a steel spike driven into the ground?

A young elephant would have no difficulty pulling the spike out or breaking the chain, yet fully-grown elephants make no attempt to escape. Why is this so?

When they are young, baby elephants are shackled for hours every day by a strong chain tied around one leg and the chain is then connected to a large block of concrete.

No amount of pulling or tugging, squealing or trumpeting will set them free. As they grow older, they learn that no matter how hard they try, it's impossible to break away from the chains. Eventually, they stop trying.

They are now mentally conditioned to believe that when a chain is placed around their leg and tethered, it's impossible to escape, no matter how light the chain or how it's anchored. If a chain is attached, they're imprisoned.

From the day we are born, we are also conditioned by our trainers. Apart from our natural instincts, we arrive with zero knowledge and everything we do or think is a result of conditioning by 'trainers' – our parents, siblings, friends, teachers, advertisements and television. Most conditioning is subtle and repetitious and enters our subconscious to be stored for decision making at a later time in our lives. While some of this conditioning is designed to keep us safe, much of it stunts our personal growth. We become tethered by mental and emotional chains. .

Our parents tell us *'Children are to be seen and not heard'*.

Our teachers tell us *'Only speak when you're spoken to'*.

Our friends tell us *'Never leave a secure job'*.

Society says, *'Pay off your mortgage and save for retirement'*.

The media tells us we're not good enough. To be happy, we must be slim, have perfect skin, hair and teeth – and smell sweet.

Their warnings are subtle and repetitious and become part of our belief system. As we grow through the steepest learning curve in our life, we are continually told what we *can't* do rather than what we *can* achieve.

Just as the elephant is conditioned to believe it can't escape, we can easily become 'can't do' people, restrained from success by repetitious negative conditioning.

The Displacement Approach

Imagine your current habits and attitudes about life are like water in a bucket. The bucket's contents have largely been filled by others – our parents, teachers, peers and the media.

Imagine now that each new skill and positive approach you've learned in this book is a pebble that you will drop into the bucket and that the water displaced represents current negative habits and attitudes. Eventually, the pebbles will displace most of the water and your bucket will be full of the positive skills, attitudes and habits that will serve you well throughout your life.

This book has given you the pebbles you'll need to relate with others on a high level, to become a more interesting, influential, magnetic person and to help people reach positive decisions. Take one skill each day and practice it until it becomes a part of who you are. It takes 30 days of repetition to form a new habit and make it permanent.

Start *now* to replace negative restraints with positive habits. How do you achieve this? The same way the elephant was trained; by repetitious learning, by continually practicing *positive* actions so that they become 'can do' habits.

References

Pease, A & B., *The Definitive Book of Body Language,* Pease International 2005,

Pease, A.V., *The Hot Button Selling System*, Pease Training, 1976

Pease, Allan & Garner, Alan, *Talk Language,* Pease International, 2004

Pease, Allan & Barbara, *Why Men Don't Listen & Women Can't Read Maps*, Pease International 2001

Pease, Allan & Barbara, *Why Men Don't Have a Clue & Women Need More Shoes*, Pease International, 2006

Pease, Allan & Barbara, *Why Men Can Only Do One Thing at a Time & Women Won't Stop Talking*, Pease International, 2003

Pease, Allan, *Questions are the Answers*, Pease International, 2003

Pease, Allan & Barbara, *How to Remember Names & Faces,* Pease International, 1996